The Dragonsitter

First published in 2012 by
Andersen Press Limited
20 Vauxhall Bridge Road
London SW1V 2SA
www.andersenpress.co.uk

2 4 6 8 10 9 7 5 3 1

British Library Cataloguing in Publication Data available.

ISBN 978 1 84939 419 2

Printed and bound in Great Britain by CPI Group (UK) LTD,
Croydon, CR0 4YY

The Dragonsitter

Josh Lacey

Illustrated by Garry Parsons

Andersen Press
London

Dear Uncle Morton,

You'd better get on a plane right now and come back here. Your dragon has eaten Jemima.

Emily loved that rabbit!

I know what you're thinking, Uncle Morton. We promised to look after your dragon for a whole week. I know we did. But you never said he would be like this.

Emily's in her bedroom now, crying so loudly the whole street must be able to hear.

Your dragon's sitting on the sofa, licking his claws, looking very pleased with himself.

1

If you don't come and collect him, Mum
is going to phone the zoo. She says she
doesn't know what else to do.

I don't want the dragon to live behind bars.
I bet you don't, either. But I can't stop
Mum. So please come and fetch him.

I'd better go now. I can smell burning.

Eddie

From: Edward Smith-Pickle

To: Morton Pickle

Date: Sunday 31 July

Subject: Your dragon

 Attachments: Poo shoes

Dear Uncle Morton,

I'm sorry for getting so cross when I wrote to you earlier, but your dragon really is quite irritating.

I hope you haven't changed your flight. If you have, you can change it back again. I have persuaded Mum to give your dragon another chance.

Luckily she didn't see him chasing Mrs Kapelski's cats out of the garden.

Uncle M, I do wish you'd told us a bit more about your dragon. You just handed him over and said he'd be fine and got back in your taxi to go to the airport. You didn't even tell us his name. And some instructions would have been helpful.

Mum and I don't know anything about dragons. Emily says she does, but she's lying. She's only five and she doesn't know anything about anything.

For instance, what does he eat?

We looked for help on the internet, but there was nothing useful.

One site said dragons only eat coal. Another said they prefer damsels in distress.

When I told Mum, she said, "Then I'd better look out, hadn't I?"

But your dragon doesn't seem so fussy. He eats just about anything. Rabbits, of course. And cold spaghetti. And sardines and baked beans and olives and apples and whatever else we offer him.

Mum went to the supermarket yesterday, but she's got to go again today. Usually one shop lasts us a whole week.

Also, you could have warned us about his poo. It smells awful! Mum says even little puppies are trained to go to the loo outside, and this dragon looks quite old, so why is he pooing on the carpet in her bedroom?

But I can see why you like him. When he's being sweet, he really is very sweet. He has a nice expression, doesn't he? And I like the funny snoring noise he makes when he's asleep.

Are you having a lovely time on the beach? Is the sun shining? Are you doing lots of swimming?

It's raining here.

Love from

your favourite nephew,

Eddie

PS. The smell of burning was the curtains. I put out the fire with a saucepan full of water. Luckily it had dried by the time Mum saw them.

Dear Uncle Morton,

I wish I could say things were better with the dragon today, but actually they're worse. This morning, we came downstairs for breakfast and found he'd made a hole in the door of the fridge.

I don't know why he couldn't just open it like everyone else. He drank all the milk and ate yesterday's leftover cauliflower cheese.

Mum was furious. I had to beg her and beg her and beg her to give him one more chance.

"I've already given him one last chance," she said. "Why should I give him another?"

I promised to help clear up any more of his mess. I think that was what changed her mind.

I'm hoping he'll go in the garden from now on.

Mum is keeping a bill for you. It's now two supermarket shops and a new fridge. She says she'll charge you for the carpet too if she can't get the stains out.

I sent you two emails yesterday. Didn't you get either of them?

Eddie

You might have to change your flights after all, Uncle M. Your dragon's done another poo in the house. This time, he couldn't get into Mum's room, because she's been keeping her door shut, so he did it on the landing right outside. I scrubbed it with bleach, but there's still a stain on the carpet. I just hope Mum won't see it. If she does, she'll ring the zoo right away, I know she will.

E

From: Edward Smith-Pickle

To: Morton Pickle

Date: Tuesday 2 August

Subject: Tethers

Attachments: Me putting out fire

Dear Uncle Morton,

What's a tether?

I don't know and Mum won't tell me, but she's at the end of hers.

That's what she says, anyway.

It was the curtains that did it.

Mum saw them last night. She was furious, but I managed to calm her down. I said I'd pay for new ones out of my pocket money.

I don't actually have any pocket money, but I promised to start saving immediately.

Also I pointed out that the hole was really quite small.

11

Mum gave a big sigh, shrugged her shoulders and stood on a chair and turned the curtains round so you could hardly see the hole. Not unless you were looking for it, anyway. And why would anyone get down on the floor and search for holes at the edge of the curtain?

Then, this morning, the dragon breathed all over them again.

It was really quite dramatic. The whole room filled with smoke. While I was running backwards and forward with a saucepan full of water (six times!), your dragon just sat on the sofa. I wasn't expecting an apology, but he could at least have looked embarrassed.

Also, he knows he's not allowed on the sofa.

This is my fifth email to you, Uncle M, and you haven't replied to one of them. I know you're on holiday but, even so, could you reply ASAP. Even if you can't come and collect your dragon, some tips on looking after him would be v much appreciated!

Edward

PS. If you don't know what ASAP means, it means As Soon As Possible.

PPS. Your bill is now: 3 supermarket shops, 2 curtains, 1 fridge, 1 rabbit, 1 new carpet. (Mum saw the stain.)

From: Edward Smith-Pickle

To: Morton Pickle

Date: Tuesday 2 August

Subject: Where are you?!!???

Attachments: Mum on the rampage

Dear Uncle Morton,

Mum rang your hotel. They said you never arrived. They said you cancelled your reservation and they gave your room to someone else.

So where are you?

Mum says you've been lying to us. She says you've always told lies, even when you were a boy, and she was stupid to think you might have changed.

I didn't know what to say, Uncle Morton. I was sure you hadn't lied to us. I don't believe you're a liar. But if you're not staying at the Hotel Splendide, why did you give us their number? Where *are* you staying?

I told Mum anything might have happened.
Maybe you banged your head and you don't
know who you are. Maybe you're in hospital,
covered in bandages, and no one knows
who to call. Maybe you've been kidnapped.
You're always talking about your enemies.
Do you need us to pay a ransom? I hope not,
because your bill with Mum is already quite
enormous.

Mum doesn't think you've been kidnapped.
Or bumped your head. She says you're
just a selfish pig and always have been,
and once you've collected your dragon she
never wants to see you again.

I'm sure she didn't mean it, Uncle M.

Little sisters are always saying stuff like
that. Emily does too. The next day, she's
forgotten what she even said.

Mum's probably just the same.

But even so, I think you should call her
ASAP.

Eddie

Dear Uncle Morton,

Mum is about to ring the zoo. She's going to ask them to take the dragon away.

I tried to persuade her not to. But she said it was the dragon or her.

I said the zoo probably wouldn't want her.

She said I should be careful because I was treading on thin ice.

I don't know what she meant, but I didn't want to ask. She had that expression on her face. Do you know the one I mean? The one that says: "you'd better keep out of my way."

So I have.

E

Dear Uncle Morton,

The zoo aren't coming. They thought Mum was joking.

When they realised she was serious, they thought she was crazy.

Finally they put the phone down.

So she rang the RSPCA, but they didn't believe her, either.

They said, "There's no such thing as dragons."

Mum said, "Come here if you want to see one."

That was when they put the phone down too.

19

Now Mum doesn't know what to do. She's threatening to kick the dragon out in the street.

I said she couldn't just leave a poor defenceless dragon out in the middle of the road where anything might happen to him.

"I've got to do something," she said. "Or I really will go crazy. What if he bites the neighbours? What if he eats one of the twins?"

It's true, he could easily pull them out of their pram. They live opposite and they're only eight months old. With teeth like his, he could gobble them up in a moment. I know you said he'd never harm another living creature, but that wasn't true, was it? What about Jemima?

Uncle M, I must have written you ten messages by now. Could you please write back?

Eddie

From: Edward Smith-Pickle

To: Morton Pickle

Date: Wednesday 3 August

Subject: Maud

Attachments: Cat attack; Mum chatting

Dear Uncle Morton,

You're not going to believe what's happened now. The dragon just attacked Mrs Kapelski's cats again. This time the garden is full of fur, and the petunias have gone up in smoke.

It was their own fault, I suppose, because they know they're not allowed in our garden. They came in anyway. They always do. They didn't see your dragon snoozing on the patio. They were rolling around on the grass when he woke up and jumped on them.

Tigger got away without any problem, but the dragon managed to grab Maud's tail in his jaws.

22

I saw it all through the French windows. I was banging on the glass, trying to make the dragon stop, but he took no notice.

Finally Maud turned round and scratched him on the nose. The dragon wasn't expecting that! He was so surprised, he opened his jaws and she was over the fence in a second. He breathed a great burst of flame after her.

Luckily he missed.

Unluckily he got Mum's petunias.

Luckily Mum didn't see what happened. She was on the phone to the pet shop. She's been ringing everyone she can think of, but no one wants a dragon.

Now she's sitting at the kitchen table with her head in her hands. She's run out of people to ring. I haven't told her about the petunias yet, but she's going to see them soon, and then I don't know what will happen.

To be honest, Uncle M, I'm a bit worried about her. I asked about mending the fridge and she said, "What's the point? The dragon will just make another hole in it."

I suppose she's right, but even so, it would be good to have somewhere to keep the milk.

Eddie

PS. You'll be glad to hear Maud is fine. She's still got all her tail.

PPS. Your dragon has spent the rest of the morning picking fur out of his teeth. He won't be attacking any more cats in a hurry.

Dear Uncle Morton,

I don't even know why I'm writing to you. You haven't answered any of my other emails. Maybe I've even got the wrong address, just like Mum's got the wrong hotel. But I've got to tell someone what's happening and I can't think of anyone else to tell.

Today was the worst day so far. Your dragon set fire to the postman.

To be fair to the dragon, I don't think he meant to. I think he must have been frightened by the letters coming through the letterbox. He breathed fire all over them. The flames went through the letterbox and out the other side, setting the postman's sleeve alight.

Luckily the postman wasn't hurt. Mum
put the flames out with a blanket. But he's
going to need a new uniform and he said
he'll charge us for it.

We had a lot of explaining to do. There was a big fire engine parked outside the house and four firemen in our front garden, wanting to check our smoke alarms.

Mum told them about the dragon. She invited them in to see him.

The firemen looked at one another in a funny way and backed down the garden path.

When they'd gone, the postman said he'd sue us. He said he'd report us to the police. He said we could expect never to get another letter in our lives. He said a lot more things which I didn't actually hear because Mum put her hands over my ears.

Now Mum's upstairs in bed. She said she'll come downstairs to make supper, but I don't know if she really will.

The dragon is lying on the sofa. I told him he should be ashamed of himself, but he doesn't look ashamed at all.

He won't get off the sofa, either. Not even when I shout at him. He knows quite well he's not allowed on there.

Eddie

Dear Uncle M

I've just been through the remains of our letters and found a postcard with a foreign stamp. Unfortunately there was nothing else left, just the corner with the stamp on, but I think the picture might have been of a beach. Did you send it to us? If you did, that's very nice of you, but it would be even nicer if you would answer my emails.

E

From: Edward Smith-Pickle

To: Morton Pickle

Date: Friday 5 August

Subject: Our tummies are empty

Attachments: The dragon in the kitchen

Dear Uncle Morton,

I am quite a long way past the end of my tether.

Yesterday I didn't think things could get any worse, but they just have.

Mum is upstairs again. She says she's not getting up till the dragon's gone. I said that might not be for three more days and she said, "Then I'm going to be spending a lot of time in bed. You'd better find me some good books."

Emily and I haven't had any breakfast and it looks as if we're not going to get any lunch, either.

Your dragon is in the kitchen. The door's shut.

He won't let me in. I just tried, but he breathed a little trickle of flame in my direction. From the expression in his eyes, I could see it was a warning.

I'm not a coward, Uncle M, but I'm not stupid, either. I ran straight out and slammed the door behind me.

I waited for a few minutes, then I peered through the keyhole and saw what he'd done.

He's been through the cupboards, smashing down the doors and tearing out all the food. He's ripped open the packets. He's chewed through the tins. There's rice and lentils and spaghetti hoops all over the kitchen floor.

Uncle Morton, what am I supposed to do?

Edward

Have you tried chocolate?

What do you mean, have I tried chocolate?

Of course I have! I love chocolate.

I don't want to be rude, Uncle Morton, but I'm beginning to worry Mum might be right about you. I've been sending you emails for almost a whole week now and I've been begging you to answer and when you finally do, you just ask if I've ever tried chocolate.

Maybe you really have banged your head!

Have you?

If you haven't, then why haven't you answered any of my other emails? Where have you been? And when are you going to come and collect your dragon?

Edward

From: Morton Pickle
To: Edward Smith-Pickle
Date: Friday 5 August
Subject: Re: Re: Chocolate

I mean, have you tried giving the dragon chocolate?

It works!!!!!!!!!!!!!!

From: Edward Smith-Pickle

To: Morton Pickle

Date: Saturday 6 August

Subject: Re: Re: Re: Re:
Chocolate

Attachments: Our very own flame-thrower

Dear Uncle Morton,

I'm sorry I haven't replied more quickly to tell you what happened, but I've been too busy feeding the dragon all the chocolate in the house and then going to the shop to get some more.

The dragon is a changed beast.

Mum says he's been behaving like a little angel and he has. He's stopped stealing food. He poos on the grass. He doesn't even sit on the sofa any more. Actually that's not quite true, but he gets off as soon as he's told to.

Tonight we had a barbecue in the garden. Your dragon lit it.

Then he ate six sausages, three chops and nine baked bananas. Luckily Mum had just been to the supermarket, so there was enough for us too.

Now your dragon is lying on the floor, looking at me with his big eyes. I know I shouldn't give him any more chocolate. I don't want him to get fat. But I'm just going to give him one more piece and then it's time for bed.

Eddie

Dear Uncle Morton,

I thought you might like to know your dragon has now eaten:

12 bars of milk chocolate

14 bars of plain chocolate

6 Twixes

1 Crunchie

and 23 bags of Maltesers.

The man in the shop is starting to look at me in a funny way.

I thought Mum would mind buying so much, but she said, "If he's happy, I'm happy."

He is. Very.

Even Emily has forgiven him. She seems to have forgotten all about Jemima. I think she'd like to have your dragon as a pet instead.

She's started calling him Cupcake.

I've told her several times that Cupcake isn't a suitable name for a dragon, but she takes no notice.

Does he actually have a name?

If he doesn't, I would suggest Desolation. Or Firebreath. Or something like that.

But not Cupcake.

I hope you're enjoying the last few hours of your holiday and managing to get a last swim and some sunshine. It's raining here.

See you tomorrow. Don't miss your flight!

Love from

Eddie

From: Morton Pickle

To: Edward Smith-Pickle

Date: Saturday 6 August

Subject: Re: Re: Re: Re: Re: Re: Chocolate

📎 **Attachments:** My island; Hotel Bellevue; Les Fruits de Mer d'Alphonse

Hi Eddie,

Very glad to hear that my tip about chocolate did the trick. It always does with dragons, even the biggest of them. I remember hiking through the mountains of Outer Mongolia with a rucksack almost entirely stuffed with Cadbury's Fruit & Nut. Without it, I wouldn't be here today. I fed the whole lot to the biggest dragon I've ever seen in my life, a bad-tempered chap with teeth as big as my hands and terrible breath.

I'll tell you the whole story when I see you, but I don't have time now. I've got to be quick. I'm in the airport and my flight leaves any minute. But I wanted to write to you and say I AM SO VERY SORRY for not reading your messages earlier in the week. I could have checked my mail at the hotel, but I had resolved not to interrupt my holiday. That was stupid of me, I know, and I am exceedingly apologetic. I only looked yesterday because I had heard a rumour from a fellow guest that there have been terrible floods in Lower Bisket, the town opposite my island. I have several good friends living there, so I wanted to check they were safe. (You'll be glad to know that the floods were actually in Upper Buckett, which is quite different.)

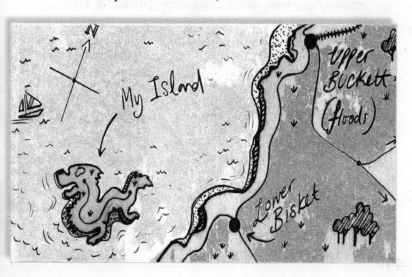

I'm very sorry too that my naughty little dragon has been behaving himself so badly. Were my instructions no use at all? I was quite sure I had included the tip about chocolate.

Will you please apologise to your mother about the mix up over hotels? I had been planning to stay in the Hotel Splendide, which is why your mother had their address and phone number. On arrival, I discovered that their chef, the famous Alphonse Mulberry, had quarreled with the owner and moved to an establishment in the next town along the coast. So I moved there too. I'm glad I did. His cooking is even more spectacular than I had remembered.

For some reason I don't appear to have your mother's email address, which is why I'm sending this to you. Please apologise to her on my behalf. I have bought her an enormous chunk of Roquefort as a present. I know how much she likes cheese.

They're calling my flight. I'd better go and join the scrum. I'll see you very soon.

Lots of love from your affectionate and apologetic uncle,

Morton

From: Edward Smith–Pickle

To: Morton Pickle

Date: Monday 8 August

Subject: ?

Attachments: Mum and her gun

Dear Uncle Morton,

I hope you had a good journey home. Did the dragon behave himself on the train?

Mum put up the new curtains and she's ordered another fridge from the shop. She says she never liked the petunias and she's decided to plant roses instead. She's going to spend the rest of your money on a new carpet for all our bedrooms.

She loves the cheese, by the way.

I don't. It smells awful. Sorry for saying so, but it does.

Emily says "thank you" for the monkey. She says he's almost as good as Jemima. I think he's even better. At least he doesn't need feeding. Also he can sleep in her bed instead of that cage at the end of the garden.

And thanks very much for the books. They'll be really useful if I ever learn French.

You know your list of instructions? Well, Mum finally found them down the back of the sofa. We've read them now. You did say the thing about chocolate, and lots of other useful stuff too. If only we'd found them before!

Mum says she thinks you just put them down there when you came to collect the dragon, but I told her not to be so silly.

Mrs Kapelski's cats have started coming into the garden again. Mum chased them out with a hose. She said, "I wish that dragon was still here." Then she looked at me very quickly and said, "I don't really."

But I think she does.

I do too.

He made everything very difficult, but he was fun too.

I hope you're having a lovely time back home on your island.

By the way, when I said I'd like to come and visit, I really did mean it.

Will you send an official invitation to Mum? Otherwise she's never going to let me.

Emily would like to come too, but I told her she's too young. She is, isn't she? She might fall off a cliff or something.

Lots of love from

your favourite nephew,

Eddie

PS. Please give Ziggy a Malteser from me.

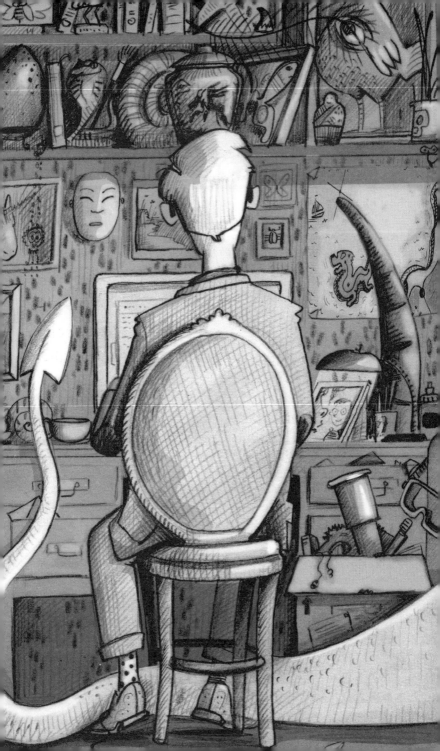

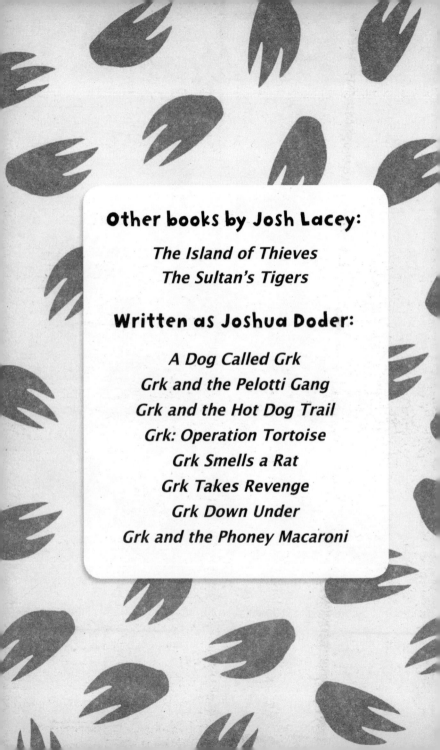

Other books by Josh Lacey:

The Island of Thieves
The Sultan's Tigers

Written as Joshua Doder:

A Dog Called Grk
Grk and the Pelotti Gang
Grk and the Hot Dog Trail
Grk: Operation Tortoise
Grk Smells a Rat
Grk Takes Revenge
Grk Down Under
Grk and the Phoney Macaroni